A Beginning-to-Read Book

A Friend for Dear Dragon

by Margaret Hillert
Illustrated by Jack Pullan

NORWOODHOUSE PRESS

DEAR CAREGIVER,

The books in this Beginning-to-Read collection may look somewhat familiar in that the original versions could have been a part of your own early reading experiences. These carefully written texts feature common sight words to provide your child multiple exposures to the words appearing most frequently in written text. These new versions have been updated and the engaging illustrations are highly appealing to a contemporary audience of young readers.

Begin by reading the story to your child, followed by letting him or her read familiar words and soon your child will be able to read the story independently. At each step of the way, be sure to praise your reader's efforts to build his or her confidence as an independent reader. Discuss the pictures and encourage your child to make connections between the story and his or her own life. At the end of the story, you will find reading activities and a word list that will help your child practice and strengthen beginning reading skills. These activities, along with the comprehension questions are aligned to current standards, so reading efforts at home will directly support the instructional goals in the classroom.

Above all, the most important part of the reading experience is to have fun and enjoy it!

Shannon Cannon

Shannon Cannon,
Literacy Consultant

Norwood House Press • www.norwoodhousepress.com
Beginning-to-Read™ is a registered trademark of Norwood House Press.
Illustration and cover design copyright ©2017 by Norwood House Press. All Rights Reserved.

LIBRARY OF CONGRESS CATALOGING-IN-PUBLICATION DATA

Names: Hillert, Margaret, author. I Pullan, Jack, illustrator.
Title: A friend for Dear Dragon / by Margaret Hillert ; illustrated by Jack Pullan.
Description: Chicago, IL : Norwood House Press, [2016] I Series: A
   beginning-to-read book I Summary: "A boy and his pet dragon make friends
   with their new neighbors, a girl and her unicorn. Completely
   re-illustrated from original edition. Includes reading activities and a
   word list"-- Provided by publisher.
Identifiers: LCCN 2015046748 (print) I LCCN 2016014720 (ebook) I ISBN
   9781599537658 (library edition : alk. paper) I ISBN 9781603578912 (eBook)
Subjects: I CYAC: Friendship--Fiction. I Dragons--Fiction.
Classification: LCC PZ7.H558 Fr 2016 (print) I LCC PZ7.H558 (ebook) I DDC
   [E]--dc23
LC record available at http://lccn.loc.gov/2015046748

288N—072016
Manufactured in the United States of America in North Mankato, Minnesota.

Come here.
Come here.
I want you to see something.

Oh, oh.
Look at that.
Do you see what I see?

Look at that man.
He is big!
What will he do?

Oh, now I see.
Here he comes with
something for that house.

Here comes a car.
Who is in it?
Can you see who is in it?

Oh, oh.
It looks like a friend for me.
Good, good.

And look, look.
A friend for you, too.
What a pretty little one.

Come on.
Come on.
Here we go.
Out, out, out!

We are happy to see you.
You look like friends for us.
That is good.
We can play and have fun.

Come on.
Run, run, run.
What fun this is!

Look at this.
See what we can do.
We like to play like this.

See, see.
He is good at this.
Look what he can do.

Yes, yes.
I see.
I see.
But we can do a good thing, too.

Look at that!
Did you see that?
That is good, too.

Look here.
This is not good.
No, no.
It is not good.

TRASH

We can help.
Get to work.
We can do this.
It will go in here.

Oh, my.
You are a big help, too.
You can get it for us.

We did good work.
Now, look here.
Look what we can have.

Oh, this is good.
We like to eat this.
We are happy.

We are happy to
have friends.
But we have to go
home now.

Here you are with me.
And here I am with you.
Oh, it is good to have friends,
Dear Dragon.

The following activities support the findings of the National Reading Panel that determined the most effective components for reading instruction are: Phonemic Awareness, Phonics, Vocabulary, Fluency, and Text Comprehension.

Phonemic Awareness: The /f/ sound

Oral Blending: Say the beginning and ending sounds of the following words and ask your child to listen to the sounds and say the whole word:

/f/ + /ish/ = fish   /f/ + /eel/ = feel   /f/ + /ire/ = fire
/f/ + /ar/ = far   /f/ + /ast/ = fast   /f/ + /an/ = fan
/f/ + /un/ = fun   /f/ + /or/ = for   /f/ + /ood/ = food
/f/ + /eather/ = feather

Phonics: The letter Ff

1. Demonstrate how to form the letters **F** and **f** for your child.

2. Have your child practice writing **F** and **f** at least three times each.

3. Ask your child to point to the words in the book that start with the letter **f**.

4. Write down the following words and ask your child to circle the letter **f** in each word:

fun   frog   family   coffee   flag   friend   leaf
raft   fan   sift   for   craft   roof   lift

Vocabulary: Related Words

1. Explain to your child that some words have many forms but the meanings are all related.

2. Write the following words on a piece of paper and explain how they are related and different, along with giving examples of each word in a sentence:

friend   friendly   friendship   befriend

3. Ask your child to describe the following:
   - A time when someone was friendly to you . . .
   - What you do to be a good friend . . .
   - Things you do to keep your friendship . . .
   - How you might befriend a new child at school or in the neighborhood . . .

Fluency: Shared Reading

1. Reread the story to your child at least two more times while your child tracks the print by running a finger under the words as they are read. Ask your child to read the words he or she knows with you.
2. Reread the story taking turns, alternating readers between sentences or pages.

Text Comprehension: Discussion Time

1. Ask your child to retell the sequence of events in the story.
2. To check comprehension, ask your child the following questions:
   - What is the man doing on pages 6–7?
   - Why did the boy and girl pick up the garbage?
   - Have you ever been the new kid at school or in the neighborhood? How did it feel? If you haven't been the new kid, how do you think it would feel?

WORD LIST

A Friend for Dear Dragon uses the 65 words listed below.
This list can be used to practice reading the words that appear in the text. You may wish to write the words on index cards and use them to help your child build automatic word recognition. Regular practice with these words will enhance your child's fluency in reading connected text.

a	eat	I	oh	us
am		in	on	
and	for	is	one	want
are	friend (s)	it	out	we
at	fun			what
		like	play	who
big	get	little	pretty	will
but	go	look (s)		with
	good		run	work
can		man		
car	happy	me	see	yes
come (s)	have	my	something	you
	he			
dear	help	no	that	
did	here	not	thing	
do	home	now	this	
dragon	house		to	
			too	

ABOUT THE AUTHOR Margaret Hillert has helped millions of children all over the world learn to read independently. She was a first grade teacher for 34 years and during that time started writing books that her students could both gain confidence in reading and enjoy. She wrote well over 100 books for children just learning to read. As a child, she enjoyed writing poetry and continued her poetic writings as an adult for both children and adults.

Photograph by Glenna Washburn

ABOUT THE ILLUSTRATOR A talented and creative illustrator, Jack Pullan, is a graduate of William Jewell College. He has also studied informally at Oxford University and the Kansas City Art Institute. He was mentored by the renowned watercolor artists, Jim Hamil and Bill Amend. Jack's work has graced the pages of many enjoyable children's books, various educational materials, cartoon strips, as well as many greeting cards. Jack currently resides in Kansas.